My Teacher's SECRET LIFE

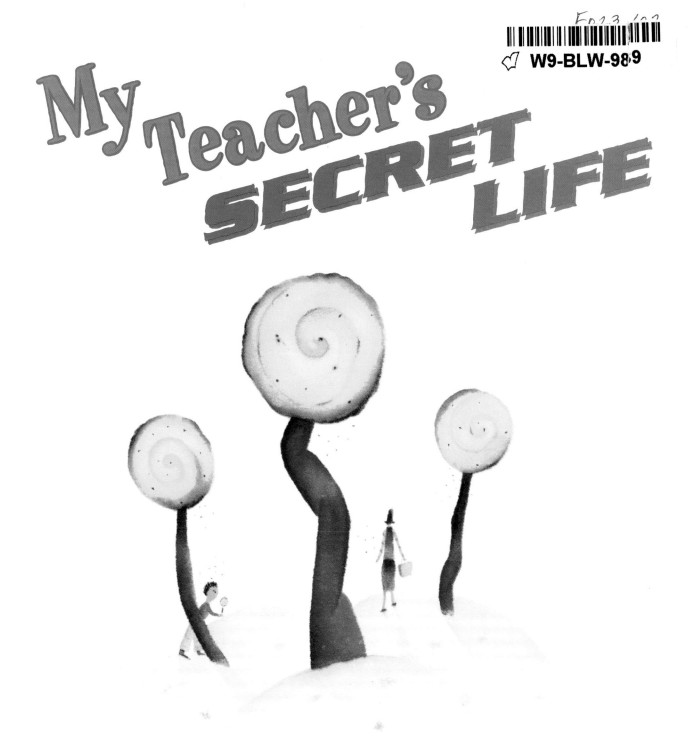

By **Stephen Krensky**

Illustrations by **JoAnn Adinolfi**

ALADDIN PAPERBACKS

First Aladdin Paperbacks edition September 1999

Text copyright © 1996 by Stephen Krensky
Illustrations copyright © 1996 by JoAnn Adinolfi

Aladdin Paperbacks
An imprint of Simon & Schuster Children's Publishing Division
1230 Avenue of the Americas
New York, NY 10020

Also available in a Simon & Schuster Books for Young Readers hardcover edition.
Book design by Paul Zakris
The text for this book was set in 17 point Cantoria
The illustrations are rendered in gouache, watercolors, pastels, and pastel pencils.

Printed and bound in the United States of America
10 9 8 7 6 5 4 3

The Library of Congress has cataloged the hardcover edition as follows:
Krensky, Stephen.
My teacher's secret life / by Stephen Krensky ; pictures by JoAnn Adinolfi.
p.   cm.
Summary: After observing his teacher at the supermarket, at the mall, and even in a park,
a young child begins to think that the teacher has a secret life.
[1. Teachers—Fiction. 2. Schools—Fiction.] I. Adinolfi, JoAnn, ill. II. Title.
PZ7.K883My   1996   [E]—dc20   95-43532   CIP   AC
ISBN 0-689-80271-4 (hc.)
ISBN 0-689-82982-5 (Aladdin pbk.)

For Joan

–S. K.

For my dearest big sister, Donna,
and my dearest big brother, James,
who always inspire me, delight me,
and care for me.

–J. A.

I know everything about my new teacher, Mrs. Quirk.
Her first name is Isabelle.
She bites her lip when she's thinking hard.
And she has eyes in the back of her head
in case we try anything funny.

Once a week Mrs. Quirk takes us
to Miss Painter's art room.
It's the only place in the school
where we can make a mess on purpose.

When Mrs. Quirk comes back,
she doesn't always recognize us.

Every day at three o'clock,
Mrs. Quirk says good-bye to us.
She doesn't have to leave, though,
because she lives at school with all the other teachers.

I can imagine what happens after we're gone.
First, Mr. Crumple, the custodian,
leads a trash patrol through the halls.
Litter, he says, is no one's friend.

Then the gym teacher, Miss Whistle,
makes everyone do exercises.

Mrs. Quirk stands in the back
because she has trouble touching her toes.

All that running around makes the teachers hungry.
The cafeteria staff cooks their meals,
putting stuff together from the lunchtime leftovers.
Potato-puff soup and macaroni bread show up a lot.

While the teachers eat, Mr. Stern, the principal,
watches closely to make sure everyone behaves.

After dinner, the librarian, Mr. Peruse, reads stories aloud.
Miss Painter covers her eyes during the scary parts.
Nothing frightens Mrs. Quirk,
but she makes faces if the story is too mushy.

Later the teachers return to their rooms.
They all keep pajamas and inflatable mattresses
in their bottom left desk drawer,
the one that locks with a key.

Sometimes the teachers have pillow fights in the hall.
Mrs. Quirk swings her pillow like a baseball bat.
The flying feathers usually make her sneeze.

At bedtime Mrs. Quirk washes her face,
brushes her teeth,
and sings a lullaby to our fish.

Sometimes she makes shadow animals
in the moonlight before she falls asleep.

Lately, though, I have been wondering
if I know Mrs. Quirk so well after all.
One Saturday I saw her in the supermarket
filling up her cart.

I wondered what she was doing.
There's always plenty of food in the cafeteria.

Then last Tuesday I saw Mrs. Quirk again,
trying on skates at the mall.
She didn't look like a teacher one bit.

I don't know what she did with the skates.
She never wears them in class or at recess.
Maybe she races down the hall late at night.

Yesterday was my biggest surprise yet.
I saw Mrs. Quirk in the park
with a strange man and a girl.
The girl looked like Mrs. Quirk, only younger.
The strange man even put his arm around Mrs. Quirk.
She didn't seem to mind.

I've been watching Mrs. Quirk extra carefully ever since.

In class she acts just the same.
She still knows who pushed who first.
And who tracked in all the mud from the playground.
And she still bites her lip while she's thinking.

Mrs. Quirk must figure she has everyone fooled.
But not me.

I know Mrs. Quirk has a secret life.
I just wonder when the other teachers
will get suspicious.